Dumpy
and the Firefighters

Julie Andrews Edwards and Emma Walton Hamilton

Illustrated by Tony Walton

HarperCollins*Publishers*

SH! SCHWEEE! SHUSS-S-S!

The sound of ice skates echoed across the frozen pond at Merryhill Farm. Almost everyone in Apple Harbor had come up to celebrate at Farmer Barnes' New Year's Day Open House.

Laughter and greetings rang in the air. Icicles hung from the rooftops, sparkling in the brilliant sunlight.

The rooster on the old barn roof watched with interest. Seldom had there been so many revelers, and certainly there was more snow than usual this year.

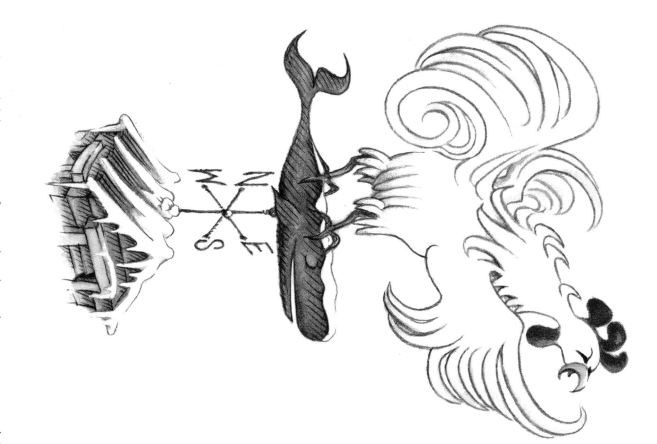

For two days, Dumpy the Dump Truck had cleared paths and made parking areas for all the guests. Charlie Barnes and his grandfather Pop-Up had worked him back and forth, snowplow attached, until there was such a pile of snow on one side that it made a splendid sled run.

Suddenly, the party mood was interrupted by a long wailing sound.

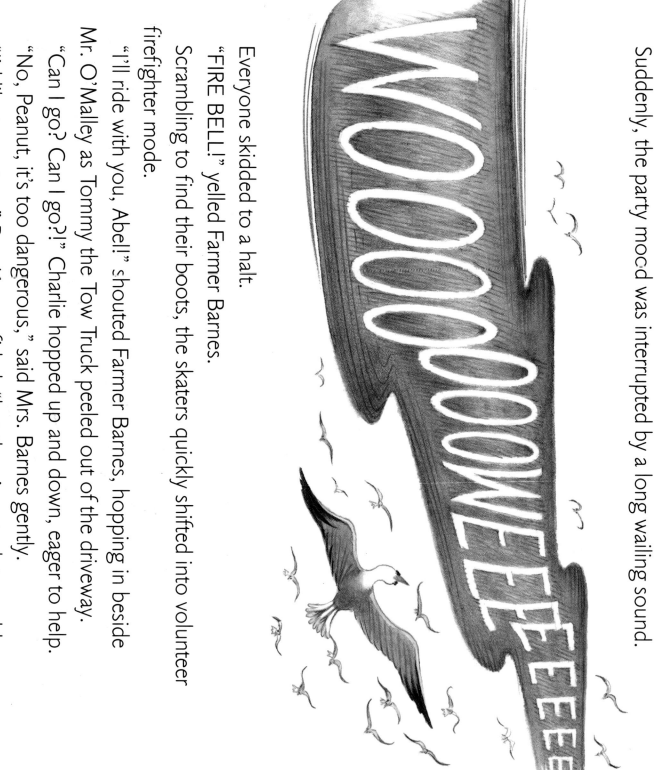

Everyone skidded to a halt.

"FIRE BELL!" yelled Farmer Barnes.

Scrambling to find their boots, the skaters quickly shifted into volunteer firefighter mode.

"I'll ride with you, Abel!" shouted Farmer Barnes, hopping in beside Mr. O'Malley as Tommy the Tow Truck peeled out of the driveway.

"Can I go? Can I go?!" Charlie hopped up and down, eager to help.

"No, Peanut, it's too dangerous," said Mrs. Barnes gently.

"I'd like to go too," Pop-Up confided, "but there's not a lot an old man and a little boy can do at a time like this."

"Look! Smoke!" Charlie pointed to a black cloud beginning to form over the village. "Maybe they need Dumpy's help!"

"Oh, darling, wonderful as Dumpy is," said Mrs. Barnes, "it's pumpers and ladder trucks they need at a fire."

"Can't I *please* just watch?"

"We could go a *little* closer, Win," Pop-Up suggested. "I promise we'll stay safely upwind."

Mrs. Barnes looked at them for a moment, then sighed.

"Be *very* careful," she said, wagging a finger at Pop-Up. "And you can drop me and all this food at the fire station."

"YAY!" Charlie shouted.

"YAY!" cried Pop-Up, and they made a dash for Dumpy.

As they neared town, the smell of smoke began to tickle their noses, and the bright sun glowed like an orange pumpkin in the darkening sky. They heard the sound of sirens behind them, and Dumpy slowed down. Big Red the Fire Engine barreled past, followed closely by Polly the Police Car.

"**WOO—WOO—WOOo!**" sang Big Red as he zoomed by. "Never a dull moment!"

"**WEE-oo, WEE-oo, WEE!**" echoed Polly.

"When there's trouble, count on **MEE!**"

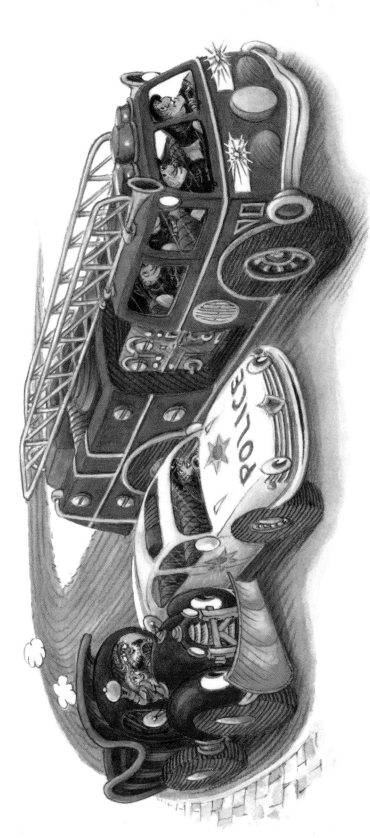

"**TOOT! TOOT!**" Dumpy called in encouragement.

Turning onto Main Street, Charlie and Pop-Up gasped. "It's Pharaoh's!" Charlie cried, and indeed, the popular general store was ablaze.

Pop-Up maneuvered Dumpy into a safe spot, and they watched Farmer Barnes, Mr. O'Malley, Ralph, and the other volunteer firefighters putting on masks, breaking windows, and attaching hose lines.

Mr. Pharaoh stood by, wringing his hands. "We were having the floors refinished," he lamented to the gathering crowd. "Maybe we left some rags too near the furnace!"

Fire exploded through the store roof. More fire engines careened around the corner, red lights twirling and sirens blaring. Firefighters from the neighboring village leaped off, uncoiling their hoses and raising ladders.

WOOOOSH!

Streams of water blasted into the sky, crisscrossing in great arcs as they attacked the raging blaze.

"WOW . . ." said Charlie, in awe.

"WOW . . ." murmured Pop-Up, equally impressed.

Dumpy trembled a little, feeling rather small beside the mighty red machines. He wished he could help.

A gust of wind caused a shower of sparks to rain down on the nearby rooftops like fireworks on the Fourth of July. More flames kindled, popping and crackling hungrily. The firefighters swept their hoses left and right, trying to protect Gianni's Barbershop and Apple Blossoms Florist, but

fanned by the wind, the fire only grew stronger.

Police Sergeant Molly Mott, using her bullhorn, reminded the anxious villagers to stay safe behind the barricades.

As the afternoon sun disappeared, it became bitterly cold. Rescue conditions worsened.

Pop-Up draped Dumpy's winter blanket across Charlie's lap, and they cuddled closer for warmth.

"Look!" Charlie cried.

"The water's freezing up!"

Within seconds, the firefighters in their big rubber boots were struggling to maintain their balance on the slippery sidewalk.

Fireman Tony sprinted past, arms full of equipment and feet desperately fighting for traction.

"Gotta break up this ice!" he yelled, and suddenly disappeared from view as he took a spectacular tumble.

Farmer Barnes and Sergeant Mott hurried over to help.

"Need a hand?" Pop-Up called.

"We need salt to melt this ice rink!" Farmer Barnes exclaimed.

"The depot's too far away. It'll take too long!" shouted Sergeant Mott.

"Sand would work as well!" Pop-Up pointed at the beach.

"How do we haul it up here?" Fireman Tony bellowed. "I can't spare a soul until we contain those flames!"

"And we can't contain the flames until we stop slipping and sliding around!" added Farmer Barnes.

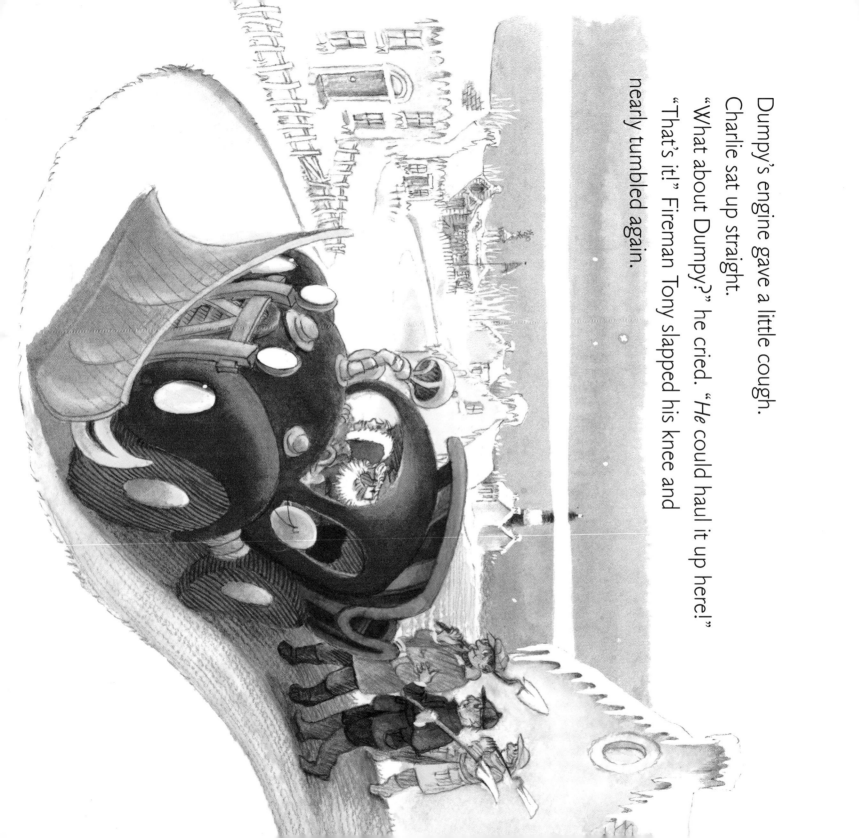

Dumpy's engine gave a little cough.

Charlie sat up straight.

"What about Dumpy?" he cried. "*He* could haul it up here!"

"That's it!" Fireman Tony slapped his knee and

nearly tumbled again.

Sergeant Mott raised her bullhorn.

"Listen up, people!" she called to the crowd. "Everybody grab a shovel and follow Dumpy!"

"**BROOM! BROOM!**" Dumpy responded as Pop-Up swung him around. The villagers fell in line, and the entire procession made its way down to the beach.

Dumpy backed onto the sand. The villagers dug in. They shoveled and swung, shoveled and swung, until Dumpy's dumper was brimming with sand.

Then, fishtailing back on the icy road, Dumpy headed for the blazing general store.

Charlie engaged the lift lever. Dumpy shuddered and groaned as he strained to lift the heavy loac skyward.

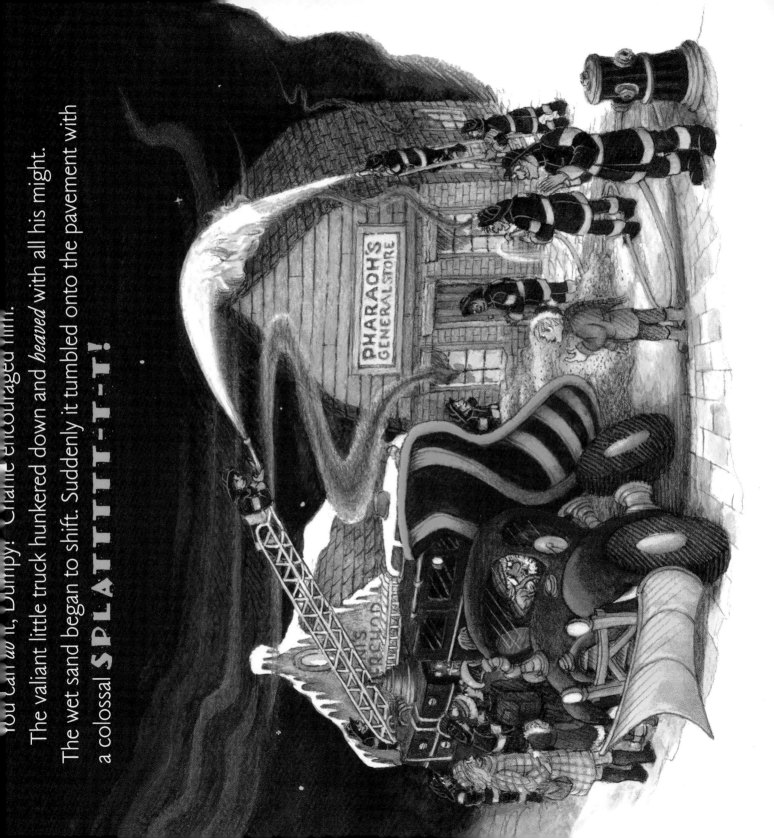

You can *do* it, Dumpy!" Crane encouraged him.

The valiant little truck hunkered down and *heaved* with all his might.

The wet sand began to shift. Suddenly it tumbled onto the pavement with a colossal **SPLATTTTT-T-T!**

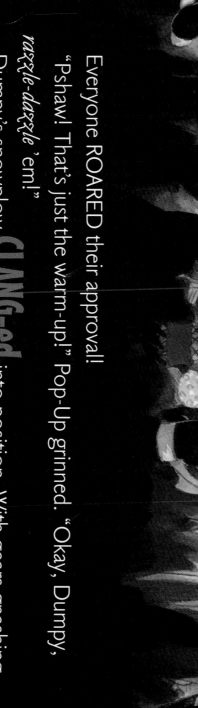

Everyone ROARED their approval!

"Pshaw! That's just the warm-up!" Pop-Up grinned. "Okay, Dumpy, *razzle-dazzle 'em!*"

Dumpy's snowplow **CLANG-ed** into position. With gears gnashing, he nosed the great mound of sand up the street and back again, until it was evenly spread along the sidewalk.

GIANNI'S BARBER

PHARAOH'S GENERAL STORE

Now, with solid footing, the firefighters could speed up their efforts.

Slowly but surely, they began to conquer the flames.

The crowd held its breath.

All at once, the fire surrendered—going out with a giant

HISSSSSSSSSSSs.

"HOORAY!"

The cheer was deafening!
As the smoke cleared, everyone could see that Pharaoh's General Store
had been spared the worst.

"Oh, Pop-Up!" Charlie was radiant. "We did it! There was something
an old man and a little boy could do after all!"

" . . . With the help of a noble dump truck!" Pop-Up beamed.

Fireman Tony dashed over, gasping his thanks.

"Come back to the station with us!" he said. "We'll hose Dumpy along with the engines and write up our report!"

After a good scrub and polish, Dumpy, Polly, Big Red, and the visiting engines were restored to their former glory.

The weary firefighters trudged indoors and discovered a marvelous feast, laid out by Mrs. Barnes and her friends.

"Mom!" Charlie ran to her. "Wait'll you hear what happened!"

Fireman Tony climbed onto a chair and raised his mug.

"A toast to Dumpy!" he declared.

" . . . *And* Apple Harbor's Bravest!" added Pop-Up warmly.

As the fireman took up his bagpipes, everyone began to dance.
Charlie could see his beloved Dumpy parked outside. The little truck's
headlights were sparkling in the moonlight, and for one magical moment,
it seemed to Charlie that he actually winked.

Dumpy's Fire Safety Tips

▶ Never play with matches or lighters.

▶ Have your parents make sure that there are smoke alarms in each room of your house, and that the batteries are checked regularly.

▶ Help your family create a fire escape plan for your home.

▶ Practice fire drills with your family.

▶ If there IS a fire, crawl UNDER the smoke.

▶ If your clothes catch fire, STOP, DROP, and ROLL.

▶ Know how to dial 911 for emergency help—and be prepared to give your full name, address, and phone number.

For Fireman Tony and Bubba Steve, with love.

Special thanks to Chief Michael F. Laffey and Tom Horn for their firefighting expertise.

Dumpy and the Firefighters • Text and illustrations copyright © 2003 by Dumpy, LLC. • Dumpy the Dump Truck is a trademark of Dumpy, LLC. Manufactured in China. All rights reserved. • www.harperchildrens.com • Library of Congress Cataloging-in-Publication Data

Edwards, Julie, date. Dumpy and the firefighters / Julie Andrews Edwards and Emma Walton Hamilton ; illustrated by Tony Walton. p. cm. — "The Julie Andrews Collection." Summary: When a fire breaks out in Apple Harbor, Dumpy the Dump Truck helps save the day. ISBN 0-06-052681-5 — ISBN 0-06-052682-3 (lib. bdg.) [1. Dump trucks—Fiction. 2. Trucks—Fiction. 3. Fire extinction—Fiction. 4. Fire fighters—Fiction.] I. Hamilton, Emma Walton. II. Walton, Tony, ill. III. Title. PZ7.E2562 Dn 2003 200201573] [E]—dc21 CIP AC

Typography by Jeanne L. Hogle • 5 6 7 8 9 10 ❖ First Edition

Color preparation by Cassandra Boyd